CHEESEBURGERS

Cheeseburgers

by

Dean Crawford

Accents Publishing • Lexington, Kentucky • 2023

Printed in the United States of America

Accents Publishing
Editor: Katerina Stoykova
Cover photo by Sean Benesh

Library of Congress Control Number: 2022951072
ISBN: 978-1-936628-97-1
First Edition

Accents Publishing is an independent press for brilliant voices. For a catalog of current and upcoming titles, please visit us on the Web at

www.accents-publishing.com

For Carol Williams, *My Brown Eyed Girl*

And many thanks to the Lexington Prose Group
for their invaluable comments.

1

Calvin Cheeseburgers invents the cheeseburger in 1872 at his restaurant in You're Now Here, Kansas. Cheeseburgers is the name of his establishment. The town's name starts out as The Middle of Nowhere, but the townsfolk think it's way too pessimistic. So they change the name to You're Now Here. The people who cling to the old name move 100 miles to the north into the only hills for hundreds of miles around to found a new town they call The Middle of Nowhere. The new location is much closer to the middle of nowhere than the old one.

Calvin is looking to settle in You're Now Here because he likes the little town. He remembers it from his days driving cattle from way down in Texas on up to Montana or Canada. The place wasn't all rowdy like Abilene or Wichita Falls. It wasn't like cowboys didn't get rowdy in You're Now Here, but they didn't shoot up the town just for the hell of it. The townsfolk were too friendly to treat them like that. There was an occasional tussle, but for the most part, the cowboys and the townsfolk got along real well.

On a bright spring day in 1872, Calvin walks from

his hotel in downtown You're Now Here west on Main Street toward the stockyards out on the edge of town. He's looking for a building suitable for a restaurant. He took up cooking on trail drives helping the cooks and learning from them, and now that he's retired from "cow pokin'", he's ready to settle down cooking in his very own restaurant. He still thinks about Hayes from time to time and wonders if the old guy is still out there on trail drives. Hayes taught him nearly everything he knows about cooking.

The town hasn't changed much, it looks pretty much the same as he remembers it. The boardwalk in front of the stores ends at Chris Craftsman's Hardware store. From there he walks along Main Street, with the horse drawn wagons of all descriptions, and people on horse back and on foot, an ox cart, and a few cows. The townsfolk are friendly. They smile at Calvin, say howdy, and the men tip their hats.

About halfway to the stockyards, Calvin sees a building on the other side of the road in a stand of trees. It's funny looking with a flat roof and stucco siding painted white. It looks like a small castle with fake turrets at the front corners of the building. He doesn't remember ever seeing it as he crosses the road for a better look, avoiding cow piles, road apples, mud puddles three feet deep, and traffic.

The building is locked up tighter than Dick's hatband. A sign hangs from the front door:

For Sale
Inquire at the You're Now Here State Bank
Main Street and Broadway.
See Mr. Henry Wilson

A faded sign painted on the front window announces the former Pappy's Wild West Cafe.

Calvin inspects the building, peeks in the windows, and makes mental notes. *The outside needs some paint, a new sign, and the grass needs cuttin'.* He can't tell much about the inside, but it doesn't look too bad. There's a well out back with a pump, and a path from the back door to an outhouse about 50 yards away in the trees. The back door is locked. The door has a window in it, and peeks in on an empty room with a door on the other side. There's a window next to the door that looks in on the empty room, too. He turns from the window and looks around. To the west on the other side of the woods is the You're Now Here Stockyards. The forest appears to go on and on behind the little place. And to the east, there ain't nothin' between there and downtown 'ceptin' some sagebrush and a tumbleweed or two.

The location is perfect, and Calvin wonders why Pappy couldn't make a go of it. The cattle trade is obviously the heart of the town's economy, and the road to the stockyards is busy. Always somebody driving cattle up or down West Main Street. Always somebody walking or riding one way or the other.

"Hey, buddy," somebody yells.

Calvin looks around and sees a scrawny old man standing on the road. The geezer is dressed in denim pants with suspenders, a plaid shirt, and boots. Long gray hair flows from under a raggedy assed cowboy hat and a long gray beard grows down his chest. The old feller reminds Calvin of Hayes, from his trail drivin' days.

"Are you talking to me?"

"I sure am, young feller. I hope you ain't thinkin' 'bout buyin' this place. Old Pappy McGee ran a great little restaurant here for years, but the Stockyard Cafe on up the road ran him out of business. It was tragic. Ike Drogue killed old Pappy, may he rest in peace. But you know, I still don't know why he would do such a thing."

"I take it that this Drogue character hanged for what he did."

"Oh no, Big Ike is top dog in You're Now Here. He does whatever he wants to. He owns the Trading Post, half of the stockyards, the Stockyard Cafe, and only God knows what else. He's a bad hombre. He's got his fingers in all kinds of evil pies. He wasn't even accused of murder much less hanged for it, but I know he did it."

"And the Stockyard Cafe is on up the road near the Stockyards?"

"That's right. It's right on up there past the Trading Post and the Stockyard Offices. You can't miss it."

The man walks off toward downtown, but he stops, turns:

"Oh yeah, people say the place is haunted. They claim Pappy still lives in there. They see lights in the building at night. They even claim to see ol' Pappy walkin' round here."

The old man walks away before Calvin can ask him anything more. He hurries out to the road to stop the old geezer, but he's gone just like that—

Calvin doesn't know what to think.

Is the old guy crazy? Or am I crazy? Should I go check out potential competition, or should I go to the bank and try to make a deal for the restaurant?

Everyone seems so friendly, the cattle even seem glad to see him, so he steps out toward the bank. The old man nags at him, but his dreams are fixin' to come true, and he's excited. He's been stashing the money he earned driving cattle for the last umpteen years in a Wichita Falls bank. But his cowboy days are over. He wants to cook in his very own restaurant.

2

Katie McGhee is up to her elbows in flour when Calvin Cheeseburgers walks by her bakery. Katie doesn't know his name, but she can see that he is tall and handsome in his denim jacket and his Stetson hat, and he's walking right on by her windows. She drops her rolling pin on the work table, wipes her hands on her apron, and runs around the counter to the door. She peeks out, but he's gone. It's the story of her life: the good-looking ones are there and gone before she can open the goddamn door.

Katie washes her hands and goes back to work. She doesn't have time to daydream about every tall handsome stranger that floats past her windows. None of them are interested in her, anyway. She's too big, too tall. She's close to 5'10" tall. She wears flannel shirts, denim pants under her apron, and she wears work boots. Her clothes hide a shapely figure, and she's stooped shouldered to hide her height from ridicule.

"Hey Baby, you sure are one long drink of water" is the one she dislikes the most. She can go on all afternoon thinking about her lack of male companionship, but the door to her shop opens, and in walks Andy Grissom, the bank messenger:

"Miz McGhee, Mr. Wilson wants you to come down to the bank. He may have a buyer for your granddaddy's restaurant."

Katie drops her rolling pin, pulls her apron off, and washes her hands. "Allison," she calls out.

"Yes, Miz McGhee," Allison responds. A young woman in her late teens comes into the room. Katie wishes she looked like Allison, who was 5 inches shorter, 30 pounds lighter, and very trim. Oh well.

"Watch the shop, Ally, while I go over to the bank." Katie starts toward the door.

"Miz McGhee," Ally says, "why don't you take off your hair net. You'll look better without it."

Katie pulls the net from her brown hair, throws it on her desk, and shakes her head to set her hair free. It's just like one of them shampoo commercials on the TV in the future she'll never see.

"Stand up straight," Ally calls out as Katie leaves.

Andy stays behind to flirt with Ally.

McGhee's bakery is all warm and cozy and sweet smelling, but You're Now Here's main street smells like fresh cow shit, aka cow piles, and horse shit, aka road apples. All of that shit negates another wise pleasant spring day. People are dodging puddles from the rain the day before yesterday, and they have to keep an eye on the mud that hasn't dried up yet. They have to watch out for cow piles and road apples as well as the traffic, which seems to keep getting worse.

Along the boardwalk, several people say hello to her.

Katie hurries along to the bank to sell Pappy's old place. She can use that money to improve her bakery, or maybe even expand it. It'll be the best bakery You're Now Here ever saw when she gets done. *Maybe that guy I saw walking by has something to do with this,* she thinks. *Maybe he'll be waiting with Mr. Wilson at the bank.* No, she shakes off the thought. *Those kinds of things only happen in the Fireside Companion.*

The old place ain't worth much, but the money will come in handy. She used money inherited from her parents to buy the bakery; she'll use some more money inherited from her grandfather to expand.

The bank is the finest building in town. It stands two stories tall at the intersection of Main Street and Broadway. Only the steeple on the 1st Congregationalist Church of You're Here Now on South Broadway is taller. Inside the bank is all wood paneling and the staidness expected of a bank. It smells clean and fresh. An armed guard wearing a uniform sits behind the Security Desk next to the front door. Iron bars protect the tellers from the customers.

"Good morning, Miz McGhee," the guard says. He tips his cap.

Katie returns the greeting.

Mr. Wilson's cubby hole is against the front window of the building. It's big enough for a desk and chair, two client chairs, a book case, and a lamp, but it's not private.

The walls don't reach all the way to the ceiling, there is no door, and the front wall facing the inside is all glass. Mr. Wilson stands up and waves to Miz McGhee when he sees her.

Katie is surprised to see the guy who walked by her windows waiting with Mr. Wilson. She wishes she had washed her face and brushed her hair. She wishes she was wearing a dress.

"Katie," Mr. Wilson says. He steps around his desk to greet her.

"Hello, Henry," she says. She offers her hand to Mr. Wilson, and he shakes it.

"Katie, this is Calvin Cheeseburgers. He wants to buy Pappy's old place. He saw it this morning."

Calvin stands up, towers over her.

Katie shakes hands with Calvin. They gaze into each other's eyes, and electricity passes between their hands like telegraph messages full of the dots and dashes of love. Katie throws her shoulders back and stands up proud and tall. Calvin is still a good six inches taller than she is. They linger over a simple handshake.

"Well," Wilson says. "I guess we better sit down and talk a little business here."

Katie and Calvin drop hands, sit down, and look at Mr. Wilson across his desk. He sits with his back to the bank's front window, and the brightness of the spring day behind him forces Calvin and Katie to look at one other again. They would have anyway, but the brightness is a good enough excuse for now.

Wilson clears his throat: "Katie, Mr. Cheeseburgers wants to buy your granddaddy's place. We've been talking a little business while we waited on you, and he's agreed to meet your asking price on the condition that he gets to see the inside of the place first."

"That's right, ma'am," Calvin says, taking over. "I couldn't see the inside very well through the windows. I'd be much obliged, Miz McGhee, if you would walk down the street with me so I can see the inside of the old place. I got some questions, too."

"He's got cash money," Mr. Wilson chimes in. "He wired it to the bank from Wichita Falls two days ago, so that it would be waitin' on him when he arrived. I think we can close the deal this afternoon, Katie. The bank can guarantee the money. Mr. Cheeseburgers has more than enough money to cover your price."

Katie looks from Calvin to Mr. Wilson and back to Calvin. She wants to sell the place in the worst way, but this man has cast some kind of spell over her. *She'll walk with him anywhere he wants to go* …

Mr. Wilson clears his throat to interrupt her reverie.

"Of course, I'll walk down there with you, Mr. Cheeseburgers. I'd be happy to. I have to stop at the bakery first to let Allison know where I'm going. It's on the way. She's probably down there flirting with Andy.

3

Katie and Calvin walk to the end of the boardwalk without a word. When Calvin tries to help her down the steps to the dirt road, she says:

"Thank you, Mr. Cheeseburgers, but I'm perfectly capable of walking."

"Yes ma'am," Calvin says, tipping his Stetson. They step out toward the old restaurant.

"Where are you from, Mr. Cheeseburgers? If you don't mind me asking, that is."

"No ma'am, I don't mind. I'm from East Tennessee. I grew up on a farm near a little ol' town called Bedbug. It ain't on any map. It's up in the Smoky Mountains in the middle of nowhere. I left there to join up with the Union Army in the war. The rest of my family was Johnny Rebs. I ain't been back."

Katie giggles.

"What's so funny, Ma'am?"

"The Middle of Nowhere is a little town about 35 miles from here."

"Oh," Calvin says. He doesn't understand.

"Well, anyway, what brings you to You're Now Here, Mr. Cheeseburgers?"

"Miz McGhee, it sure would please me if you'd call me Calvin."

"Okay, Calvin, but only if you call me Katie."

"It's a deal," he says. They shake hands on it, and the electricity is still there.

"So, why is a man from Bedbug, Tennessee buying a restaurant in You're Now Here, Kansas?"

"This ain't the first time I been here, ma'am ... I mean, Katie. I was on some of them cattle drives that stopped out there beyond the stockyards. We came into town to buy supplies, wet our whistles, and sometimes to do some livestock trading. I remember this place being right friendly, but I don't remember your granddaddy's restaurant. I don't guess I was ever in it. What about you, Katie. Where are you from?"

Before Katie can reply, they're crossing the road dodging cow piles, road apples, mud puddles, and horse drawn vehicles to the former Pappy's Wild West Cafe. Katie takes a ring of keys from a pocket, finds the key to the front door, and opens it. She follows Calvin into the building.

Calvin examines the walls looking for cracks. The white paint is faded, but he doesn't find any problems. The roof isn't leaking, because the ceiling looks good. He's gonna have money left over after writing Katie a check.

He looks over the stove and opens the oven and the icebox. They all need cleaning, but otherwise they look okay. He'll have to ask Katie where the icehouse is.

The dining room is dirty, cobwebs fill every corner, and dust bunnies litter the floor tumbling on the least of air currents. Some of the tables and chairs will have to go, but the rest are okay, or at least can be fixed. Dust covers every flat surface. He'll have to dust, sweep, and mop. *Surely Katie can direct me to where I can buy cleaning supplies.*

The air in the place is stale, and the room smells musty. He'll have to open the doors and windows and give the place a good airin'. A good scrubbin' will help, too.

He finds two rooms in the back side by side. One is obviously a storeroom because it doesn't have any windows. The other room has two doors and a window. It's an office, no doubt. He crosses the room to the back door, unlocks it, and opens it. A path leads out to the outhouse, and the well and pump are to the left. He closes the door and locks it again. *I'll have to ask Katie about this room.*

After his inspection, and after Katie answers all of his questions, Calvin is almost ready to buy the restaurant, but he's got one more question. "An old guy told me this morning that this place is haunted. He said Pappy is still living here. What do you know about that?"

"Yes, I've heard that, but surely you don't believe in ghosts, do you?"

"I don't know, Katie, I've seen some pretty strange

things out there on the trail with a herd of cattle. Ever seen St. Elmo's fire on the horns of a herd of cows? It's downright spooky."

"No, I haven't, but if you think the place is haunted, you can back out of this deal right now, and I won't think any the worst of you."

"Oh no, ain't no ghost gonna scare me off. I been chomping at the bit to settle down with a nice little restaurant of my own, and this looks like the right place to me."

Calvin is seeing Katie in a new light now that he has taken care of business. She's right attractive. Especially when she stands up tall and straight. He likes tall women since he's tall. For some reason she's hiding a nice figure under all that flannel and denim. *Hmm. I'm gonna have to look into that.*

"Well, Miz Katie, I'm ready to go back to the bank and write you a check."

Katie locks up the old building, and they step out toward the bank.

"There's a room back there that looks like it could be an office. How did your granddaddy use that room?" Calvin asks.

"He had a desk in there, but Granny took care of the business end at home until she died. Then I took over for her. I was managing his restaurant at fifteen, and I was workin' there and learnin' about baking and cooking. And I was going to school."

"You were a busy little girl, Katie."

"Pappy lived in that room after Granny died. He had it set up like a bedroom. I've still got the furniture he had in there. I'll be glad to let you have it. Well, maybe not the old cot, but I've got a bed you can have."

"Katie, were you born here in You're Now Here?"

"No, I was born in Chicago, but I came here to live with my mother's parents when I was five. My parents died together in a fire. My mother grew up here and went to school here. She met my father at the University of Illinois. He was from Chicago. When I was old enough to collect the money my folks left me, I bought the town's only bakery. That's when I was eighteen. I've been running it ever since."

"Did you ever live in the restaurant?"

"No, I lived in my grandparents' house. I still do. It's right around the corner from the bank on North Broadway. I inherited it when Pappy died. My grandmother died when I was fifteen. The doctor said she had consumption. She wasted away. It was just awful"

"I'm sorry," Calvin says.

"When grandma died, Pappy started spending more of his time at the restaurant. He moved into that little room. After I bought the bakery, I didn't see him for days sometimes."

And that's all the conversation they could work in walking back to the bank.

4

Katie McGhee's image breaks up into jagged little pieces like a kaleidoscope in Calvin's head, and then reassembles over and over in vignettes from the walk down to the restaurant and back. Snippets of conversation repeat themselves. If he didn't know better, he'd say some locoweed got into his feed. When they get back to the bank and the deal is done, Calvin doesn't want to say goodbye to Katie. He has to think quick, or she she'll walk right through that door and out of his life.

"Katie," Calvin says, catching up to her at the bank's front door.

Katie turns from the door: "Yes, Calvin."

"Can you tell me where to buy some furnishings for my room? I want to settle in as soon as possible and get that place up and runnin'. Not to mention the hotel bill I'm runnin' up."

Katie smiles at him. "I think I can help you out. I've got a house right around the corner. It's full of old furniture. I'm sure we can decorate that little old room in no time. But first I gotta check in at the bakery."

"I'll go to the hotel and check out while you're doin' that," Calvin says.

5

Right around the corner on North Broadway is the edge of You're Now Here. An alley runs behind the buildings on Main Street to service them. Katie's house faces Broadway about twenty yards from the alley. She wore a path from the back door of her house to the back door of the bakery. Across North Broadway, three small houses sit empty in disrepair. Beyond them there isn't another building on the road for 35 miles. North Broadway is the road to The Middle of Nowhere.

"Katie, you shore got yer self a nice house here," Calvin says.

They're standing in front of her house after a short walk from the bakery. It's a wood frame house, two stories, with clapboard siding painted white. The house is shaped like an L if one could fly over like a big bird and look down on it. The front porch is big enough for several people to sit and rock and wave to people walking by the house, or riding on a horse or in a wagon—except nobody ever walks or rides by. Broadway is developing to the south of Main Street.

"So you inherited this place from your Grandparents?"

"That's right. Pappy bought the house and 55 acres

from the family that built it. It's almost 70 years old. There wasn't anything here at the time. Some of the townsfolk like to say the house was built in the middle of nowhere until The Middle of Nowhere moved 35 miles to the north."

Katie chuckles, but her humor escapes Calvin again, hops right over his head. He enjoys standing in the shade of two big maple trees listening to her talk, though. He doesn't care what she says. Her voice is sweet and angelic. Her laugh is the trill of a song bird.

"Did your Pappy ever farm this place?"

"Oh, he grew some vegetables for his restaurant, but he was into cooking, not gardening. After he died, I was too busy running my bakery to grow veggies. He didn't like cattle. He did go fishing a lot at a little pond out there in the middle of the woods. He would camp out for a day or two sometimes."

Katie falls silent remembering her grandfather.

Then she says, "Well, I guess we better go inside and find you some furniture for that room of yours, I've got everything Pappy had in that little room stored in my attic."

Calvin follows Katie into the house and up to the second floor. He can't help but notice she needs tighter pants. She's got a nice ass. Wow, he wants to reach out and touch it like he would if she was a whore. He played grab ass with many a whore on the stairs, but he didn't think he oughta with a respectable business woman. He hasn't felt this way about a woman before, and he doesn't know how to court a woman like Katie. He can't even remember the last time he met a respectable woman. What in the world is he going to do to impress her?

The attic is an unfinished second floor room. Katie chooses the furniture, helps Calvin carry it down to the front porch, and then takes him to the barn out behind the house where she harnesses a team of mules to a flat bed wagon. He tries to do it for her, but she pushes him away. He's never known a woman to do such a thing.

She drives the wagon back to the house and helps Calvin load the furniture on it. Katie drives the wagon and its load right down Main Street big as you please with Calvin sittin' right up there next to her on the seat.

«——————————————————————»

Calvin gathers some brush, starts a fire in the stove. Katie pumps a five gallon pail full of water and puts it on the stove. They clean the room within an inch of its life using cleaning supplies Katie brought along.

"You'll have to buy your supplies at Henderson's General Store and Trading Post, Calvin. The You're Now Here Trading Post is owned by Ike Drogue. I don't do business with the man. He's a evil, Calvin. Don't get mixed up with him."

He doesn't even know this Ike Drogue fella, and already he doesn't like him. When he asks about the guy, she turns their conversation to other topics while they work.

Katie helps him unload the furniture and decorate his room. She places the head of his bed against the outside wall so that it sticks out into the room, but not enough to interfere with traffic from the front door to the back door. A nightstand sits between the bed and the window in the rear wall. On the other side of the bed, she places a chiffon robe, chest of drawers, and a small roll top desk side by side against the inside wall. Small rugs are on the floor on either side of the bed, and a runner runs from the front door to the back one. Blue and white checkered curtains go up over the window in the door and the window next to it. A wash stand stands next to the back door with a bowl and pitcher on top, and a towel hanging from the front of it.

When they're finished, Calvin sits down on the bed Katie insists on giving him. She made it up with a wedding ring quilt on top. The room may be too fancy for Calvin. He can't remember living in such a splendor, certainly not in Bedbug, the army, or trail drivin'.

Katie sits in a chair at the roll top desk and talks about the old days when cowboys drove cattle right down Main Street, and parents had to keep their kids out of the road.

Calvin is not keeping up with the conversation very well because he's thinking about Katie. She's a mule skinner, a stevedore, a decorator, and a baker. She's everything a man could want. And she's pretty and has such a nice figure. *I wonder why she hides it?*

"Well, Katie, you're shore one amazing woman. I'm much beholden to you. Why don't you let me buy you a dinner? What about the Stockyard Cafe? An old guy said something about it this morning while I was looking this place over for the first time."

"I don't frequent that place, and I never will," she says. "Ike Drogue owns it."

"Well, how about the Hotel Dining Room? I ate there last night and this morning. Both meals tasted pretty good to me."

"I don't know, Calvin, that's awful expensive. I could cook for us at my house."

"Then you will have dinner with me," Calvin says.

"Why, of course. I really like you, Calvin. I've had a real good time with you this afternoon."

"Well you been working hard today. Why don't you go on home and pretty yourself up, and we'll let somebody else do the cookin' tonight. Whaddya say?"

"Listen, I'm sorry we can't go to the Stockyard Cafe 'cause it would be cheaper than the Hotel Dining Room, but I hate Ike Drogue.

"Why do you say that?"

"I think Ike murdered my grandaddy, but I don't have any proof."

"What happened?"

"Ike found Pappy dead, face down in a pen out at the stockyards about two years ago. The Sheriff ruled it accidental. He didn't even bring in the coroner. There was no inquest or anything. I tried to get Sheriff Trover to investigate, but he declined. He said the case was closed like maybe he was afraid of ol' Ike."

"You know, the old guy on the road this morning told me that he knew that Ike killed your granddaddy. He didn't say how he knew, and before I could get any more information out of him, he was gone."

"What do you mean he was gone?"

"I was standing outside near that back corner." Calvin points in that direction. "By the time I got out to the road to talk to him some more, he was gone. It was like he disappeared into thin air."

"What did this man look like?"

Calvin describes him, and Katie's face drains of color. She looks away from him.

"Katie, are you okay? Katie."

"I'm sorry, Calvin, I don't know what came over me. Look, if we're gonna eat tonight, I'd better get home and start cookin'. You will come to my house for dinner, won't you?"

"I thought we were going to the Hotel Dining Room," Calvin says.

"That's right. Well, I better get on home and get ready. Listen, I can come back and get you around 7."

"Thank you, but that ain't much of a walk to your place, and the Hotel is close by. I'll walk. It's no problem at all."

"You don't still have a room rented there, do you?"

"Oh no ma'am, I checked out of the Hotel this morning."

"Okay, I'll see you around 7."

Katie stands up and so does Calvin. He walks with her through the back door to her wagon, where her mules wait patiently. Katie kisses Calvin lightly on the cheek before she climbs up in the wagon and drives off. She waves at Calvin, and he waves back. He follows her to the corner of the building and watches her turn right onto Main Street and drive away.

Calvin has never felt so empty. Somebody just yanked the life out of him by the roots. He hasn't known this woman 24 hours, and already she's everything to him. The inside of his head turns round and round. *What has she done to me?*

6

Calvin Cheeseburgers is about the nicest man to come along in a month of Sundays. The afternoon takes on an urgency Katie hasn't felt in a long time. Not since Randy moved to The Middle of Nowhere. She's going to drag out the wash tub to clean up for this man. If she's going to give herself to him, and she is, she's going to be clean from head to toe. *I hope he takes a bath. On the other hand, giving him a bath is a pretty good idea …*

"Slow down, girl, you're movin' way too fast."

"Oh, hi Granny, where you been? I ain't seen you in a while."

"Ain't been nuthin' happenin' here," Granny says. She's a hip granny wearing tight jeans, a fancy embroidered cowboy shirt with the tail out, a cowboy hat, and blue and white cowboy boots. Her gray hair is short. She looks 20 years younger than she was when she died. She's holding a martini in one hand and a cigarette in the other.

"Ain't no use me hanging around here if you don't need me. I lived in this town once, remember? You're Now Here is about as exciting as watching paint peel off a wall, as I recall." She takes a puff and then a sip.

"Well, I'm goin' to dinner tonight with a man. We're

goin' to the Hotel Dining Room. I tried to talk him into letting me cook for him, but he said I had worked too hard today. Wasn't that nice of him? I'm all excited. I gotta feeling about him. He could be the one."

"I can't leave you alone for a minute, can I? You were always boy crazy. How many times have I told you to stop flirtin' with them boys?"

"Granny, I'm not 15 years old anymore. I'm a grown up woman, and Calvin is a grown man. We can do whatever we want, and I sure hope he wants to."

"I'm sorry, dear, I keep forgetting. So tell me about this feller."

"Calvin is a dreamboat, Granny. He's tall and strong and polite and kind and sexy—"

"Hold it, I get the picture. You got the hots for this guy."

"Whatever are you talkin' about?"

"I'm sorry, dear, you're attracted to this guy."

"Oh, my God, I fell in love with Calvin at first sight. We shook hands in Mr. Wilson's office, and I could feel the electricity. I just spent a wonderful afternoon with him. Oh, and by the way, I sold Pappy's restaurant to him."

"Well, thank God, maybe he'll move out of that place now."

"Somebody's told Calvin about the place being haunted, and I think it was Pappy he described. It sure sounded like Pappy. Will you talk to him? I really like

Calvin. I'm head over heels in love with him. I can't believe how wonderful I feel. Tell Pappy not to chase him off."

"Okay, Girl, I'll talk to him, but you know Pappy's stubborn as a team of old mules, and I guess he always will be, but I'll see what I can do. I guess I better get on out of here. I hope you get lucky tonight, Katie."

"Get lucky? What does that mean? You talk strange these days."

"I'm sorry Katie, it's the time difference. On this side, there ain't no time. Takes a little gettin' used to, but once you do, it's a groove. What I meant to say was 'good luck with your new man.' Ta ta."

7

Calvin Cheeseburgers knocks on Katie McGhee's front door at 7:00 according to the pocket watch, a Riverside Waltham he won in a poker game in Billings …

… he recalls how he emptied the bucket Katie left behind, filled it, rinsed it out, filled it again. This time he carried the pail to his kitchen where he rekindled the fire from earlier. When the water got warm, he bathed as best he could with one of the washcloths Katie gave him along with towels, sheets, pillows, pillow cases, hangers, and what not—firewood became a priority hoppin' around naked tryin' to get clean, hopin' the whole dang town ain't watching him—rinsed with water gone luke warm, shivering, freezin' his ass off.

He worries he's still not clean enough for her when he knocks on her door. He's wearing his only clean shirt and pants, his Stetson, and his new cowboy boots.

Katie answers the door smiling, bubbly, and excited. She's wearing her Sunday finest gingham dress, brown high button shoes, and her hair piled up on her head. Calvin is flustered. He's never seen a woman anywhere between San Antone and You're Now Here as gorgeous as this woman. Words like wow, gee whiz, and good golly, stammer out of his mouth and fall flat at his feet. *This is an intelligent woman, a real woman, and I'm afraid I'm gonna say something stupid.*

When it's obvious to Katie that Calvin has fallen under some sort of spell, she takes him by the hand and walks with him to the Hotel You're Now Here. He lets her take the lead, because he has no idea of how to proceed with this woman.

He remembers eating fried chicken, mashed potatoes and gravy, green beans, fried corn, tomatoes, cucumbers, corn bread, and drinking lots of unsweetened ice tea. The Hotel Dining Room puts on quite a spread. He remembers talking to her more than he's talked to anyone in years. By the time they get back to her house, she knows more about him than anyone dead or alive.

He will always remember making love to her that night back at her place—because it is their first time, and because he never knew sex could be so sweet. With whores, it was all wham, bam, thank you, man, next; but he knows he isn't playing a fiddle anymore. He has a violin in his hands now. She is soft and curvy, and she guides him to all the right places, all the right spots, and she rocks and rolls with him all over the bed until they are both spent and collapsed in each other's arms. They fall asleep like a couple of spoons.

When a rooster wakes him up a little after sunrise, Calvin knows for sure he's in love. He figures as much before drifting off to sleep cuddled with Katie, but now it's official because he doesn't want to get dressed and sneak away. He wants to wake her up and talk about what happened last night. He wants to talk about their future together. He wants to talk about things he has never talked about with a woman before.

When the rooster crows some more, Katie wakes up. Calvin is sitting on the bed naked, Indian like, legs crossed in front of him, arms crossed over his chest, gazing at her.

Katie is startled but recovers quickly and smiles at Calvin. "Good morning, sweetheart," she says.

"I love you, Katie," Calvin says

"I love you too, Calvin." She giggles.

"I want to be your man, and I want you to be my woman."

"Are you proposing marriage, Cal?"

"I guess I am, cause I sure do like wakin' up next to you in the mornin', and I want to keep on doin' it."

Katie grabs him, pulls him down on the bed, and accepts his proposal over the next 15 or 20 minutes with lots of enthusiasm.

8

Katie McGhee goes through her morning routine on a fluffy white cloud of flour. Never in her life has she felt like this before. Randy never did anything for her like this, which is why she wasn't all that upset when he went on down the road to The Middle of Nowhere. But if Calvin Cheeseburgers were to up and leave town, that would be a different story. She'd go after him, rope him, hog-tie him, and carry him back on home. *I'm gonna marry him—*

"Miz Katie."

Allison's voice interrupts Katie's reverie. "Yes."

"Where are you this morning, ma'am? You certainly aren't here."

Katie giggles and spills it all to Allison, including Calvin's proposal and her acceptance.

"Whaddya mean you're gonna get married? You just met the guy yesterday. Don't you think you're rushing into this?"

"Listen, Ally, I ain't gettin' any younger. I'm almost 25. There ain't any eligible bachelors in this town; you know that. I ain't movin' to Abilene or Salina to find me a husband when I got a man right here right now wantin' to marry me.

"I take it then you ain't gonna marry Big Ike."

Katie stops kneading a ball of dough and looks at Ally. "Lordy girl, how many times have I told you I ain't marryin' Big Ike Drouge. He's old enough to be my grandpa. I told him I ain't gonna marry him at least ten thousand times, and that's no exaggeration. He just keeps comin' back. I don't know what's wrong with him—Well, yes I do. He's a murderer for one thing, but besides that, he's just downright evil."

"It'll be a good thing to have Calvin around," Ally says.

"What do you mean?"

"Well, surely Big Ike will quit comin' around after you and Calvin get married."

"I never thought of that. I mean, I've fallen head over heels in love with Calvin. Ain't nothing like this ever happened to me before. I ain't had time to think about it all."

"I hope you're not makin' a big mistake, Katie."

"I love him, Ally, I knew it when we met in the bank yesterday. There was electricity between us. I feel really good about this."

9

Calvin Cheeseburgers thinks about Katie while driving her wagon and mules down South Broadway to Henderson's General Store and Trading Post. He can't wait to see her again. She lets him hitch the mules up to the wagon since he is borrowing the mules and the wagon. They kiss and hug out at her barn like they're never going to see each other again. Parting is such sweet sorrow, although the official word hasn't reached You're Now Here yet.

Katie warns him not to shop at the You're Now Here Trading Post. "I don't do business at Big Ike's. Henderson's isn't hard to find. It's less than a quarter mile away on South Broadway. You can't miss it. There are only three or four stores down that way."

Thank God neither one will live long enough to see the You're Now Here Walmart/Lowe's complex with parking for thousands, complete with a McDonald's, a Pizza Hut, and a Chili's out front by the street.

«———————————————————————»

Calvin unlocks the back door of his new restaurant and carries his cleaning supplies to the storage room.

Then he walks in the woods around the building collecting firewood.

He starts a fire in the stove. He heats water in a five gallon galvanized pail, stirs in soap powders, and washes out the icebox with a sponge. Then he brings in a block of ice from the wagon and places it in the bottom of the box. On his last trip to the wagon, he unhitches the mules, tethers them nearby to graze, and takes in the little bit of food he bought for his lunch and two bottles of root beer to the icebox.

Calvin resumes his cleaning. He washes walls, the storeroom, the oven, the counter top, table tops, and chairs. He takes several chairs to the storeroom. Some of them may be beyond repair, but there's hope for a few. He goes at it hard and steady until he needs a break. He's going to mop the floors when he's had a rest. Then he'll cut grass while the floor dries. He sits down at a table against the front window. He watches traffic move along on West Main Street and thinks about Katie some more.

"Well, I see you bought the place."

Calvin jumps and turns in his chair. It's the old man from yesterday morning. "Damn, you scared me. I didn't hear you come in."

"I thought I warned you against it. Big Ike ain't gonna like it that you're gonna open this place again. He'll be sending a welcoming committee."

"Why is Big Ike so afraid of competition? Surely he doesn't think I'm gonna run him out of business."

"Big Ike thinks Pappy buried a treasure here under the floor."

"Did he?"

"Hell no, Pappy wasn't stupid. He put all of his money in that bank down there on the corner. He earned a lot letting the bank invest his money. He had plenty to take care of his family, but they didn't put on no airs, so nobody ever thought of them as rich. A legend quickly grew up about a treasure Pappy hid somewhere. It was the gold he mined in Californie according to the legend."

"Ike's been trying to marry Katie ever since Pappy died," the old man continues. "He's already turned the restaurant inside out lookin' for it. Now he thinks it's buried out there on that farm, and he wants to marry Katie so he can get hold of the place."

The old guy chuckles.

"But he put it in the bank, right?"

"Oh, hell yes. Pappy believed in banks. He made a lot of money out in Californie after the '49 gold rush. He didn't live like no rich man, so some people think he settled here because he ran out of money on his way back home to Kentucky. Others said he had lots of money and buried it somewheres for safe keepin'. They said he didn't believe in banks, which is road apples. Go down there and ask that Henry Wilson. He'll tell ya. I understand Katie inherited all that money. She'll make some lucky man a fine wife."

This mention of Katie makes Calvin suspicious. The

old man seems to know that he knows Katie. And how would this old coot know about their plans to marry?

"Say, old timer, what did you say your name is?" Calvin asks.

"I didn't say, young feller, and I don't think I like yer attitude."

The old man turns and walks away. Calvin gets up and goes after him. He reaches for the old man's right arm and gets nothing but air. The old man turns translucent and then disappears altogether by the time he gets to the back room.

Calvin stops dead in his tracks, blinks, then rubs his eyes. *Am I going crazy? Is someone slipping locoweed into my feed? What the hell is going on?*

Two big burly guys emerge from the back room. They're each as tall as Calvin, but they each outweigh him by 50 or 60 pounds. They're wearing denim pants, flannel shirts, cowboy boots, and they're totin' guns in holsters on belts slung around their waists.

"Are you Calvin Cheeseburgers?" one of them asks.

"Who wants to know?" Calvin replies. He backs away toward the front door, still reeling from his encounter with the old man.

"The boss wants to see you."

"Who is this boss, and what if I don't want to see him?"

"Big Ike told us to bring you to him whether you wanted to go or not." One of the guys draws a Colt .45

Frontier Special and points it at Calvin. The other guy does the same.

"Big Ike told us to bring you in dead or alive. I don't particularly like killin', but hey, I'm not going to horse around with you."

Big Ike is a little guy. He's about 5'3" tall and a real lightweight. How he got to be Big Ike is not apparent to Calvin, who thinks the guy looks pathetic behind his big ol' desk in his great big ol' office tryin' to look mean. His forehead dominates his face because of a receding hairline. A black bandito mustache is waxed and curled at the ends. His face is oval shaped and red. His eyes are jet black and evil.

"I'm surprised you bought that old place after we tore it up lookin' for Pappy's treasure. So, what have you found down there?" Big Ike wants to know. "Did you find the treasure?"

"I ain't been looking for no treasure, and the place doesn't look torn up to me."

"Oh. I guess ol' Pappy fixed it up again. I heard he was living down there. People say they see lights in that ol' building at night. Have you met him yet, Mr. Cheeseburgers?

When Calvin doesn't reply, Big Ike continues.

"We didn't find it, and you say you didn't find it, so the treasure must be somewhere on that farm. People been diggin' round out there for years, even before ol' Pappy died. You been courtin' the granddaughter, haven't you?"

Apparently, it's a rhetorical question, because Big Ike doesn't give him a chance to answer.

"Well, I don't like it. And don't think you're gonna romance that treasure, 'cause you ain't. That treasure is mine. I'm gonna marry her. You understand me, Mr. Cheeseburgers?"

"No, I sure don't, Mr. Drogue. I sure don't. I asked Miz Katie to marry me, and she said yes. She didn't say anything about her marryin' up with you." Calvin wants to use his arms and hands for emphasis at this point, but his arms are tied behind him at the wrist, a piece of rope is biting into him.

Big Ike swells up out of his chair, face turning redder, mouth snarling mad dog like. He walks around his desk and plants himself in front of Calvin.

"Look, I don't like you, Mr. Cheeseburgers—"

He has to stop because Calvin tries to kick him. Big Ike backs away. The thugs pull Calvin backwards out of kicking range, twisting the rope around his wrist tighter.

Big Ike yells, "As a matter of fact, I hate your fuckin' guts. I don't like that you've come to my town. I don't like it that you're messin' with my fiancée. I want you to leave. I want you gone by sundown. Got that, cowboy? 'Cause if you don't go, I'll have you killed. I might even do it myself."

"I ain't goin' nowhere, Mr. Drogue," Calvin says. "I

bought myself a restaurant yesterday, and I will open it. I don't know anything about a treasure. And as far as Katie McGhee is concerned: if you hurt her in any way, I'll hunt you down like a mad dog and put a bullet right between your eyes. You got that, Mr. Big Ike?"

Amused by his defiant stance, Ike Drogue smiles at Calvin. "Boys, take Mr. Cheeseburgers out back and change his mind about staying around here. Good bye, Mr. Cheeseburgers, it was nice knowin' ya."

Big Ike's thugs literally drag Calvin out of the office. They drag him out behind the Stockyard Cafe and beat the shit out of him. One of them holds Calvin from behind, while the other punches him in the face, chest, and stomach. Calvin struggles, but the men are too big and strong. They leave him on the ground near unconscious and go back to Big Ike's office.

A man steps out of the shadows of the building and bends over Calvin.

"Hayes?" Calvin whispers.

10

Calvin wakes up in his bed in the back room of his restaurant with Katie hovering over him. His head hurts, his ribs hurt, and his stomach hurts. He can't see very well through swollen eyes, but he makes out Hayes behind her sitting at the roll top desk.

"Calvin, are you all right?" Katie says when she sees his eyes open. "Who did this to you? Dr. Smith is on his way. I'm so sorry, darling. When I find out who did this, I'm gonna shoot the sorry asshole."

"It was Ike's thugs," Hayes speaks up. "I don't know their names, but I seed it all out behind the Stockyard Cafe. I was out there takin' a smoke."

Hayes is a short, scrawny little guy with a beard and long gray hair flowing from under a worn out cowboy hat that may have been a Stetson at one time or another.

"What was Calvin doin' there?"

Calvin tries to sit up and defend himself, but his head threatens to burst open, and he eases back down on the pillow. His face is puffy and bruised.

"I don't know what he was doin' there," Hayes says. "Hell, I ain't seen ol' Cal in a couple of years, at least."

"So you know Calvin."

"Oh, yes ma'am, me and him worked on cattle drives together. He wanted to be a cook, so he hung out with the cooks every chance he got. I taught him a considerable amount about cookin'."

"What's your name, and what were you doing at the Stockyard Cafe?"

"I'm Hayes, and I work there, ma'am. I'm a cook."

"How did you know to bring him here?"

"I heered people talkin' about him buyin' this place. I figured he was livin' here like Pappy did. I wish I could have stopped 'em, but I'm an old man, and they would have beat me too. We'd both still be up there face down in the dirt."

"Did you know Pappy?"

"Yes ma'am, I met him about a year before he died. I used to come down here and drink and play cards with him from time to time. He was a good ol' feller. I was right sorry about his passin'."

"I'm his granddaughter, Katie.

"Well, I sure am pleased to meet you, ma'am. Pappy talked about you a lot. I wish I could stay and talk to you longer, but I gotta get on back to the café, or Big Ike will be firin' me again."

When Hayes is gone, Calvin tries to sit up in the bed. He wants to talk, but Katie pushes him back down.

"You've got to rest up, Cal, you've been hurt pretty bad. Dr. Smith will be here any minute."

And on cue, Dr. Smith knocks on the back door, opens it, and walks right in.

11

Dr. Smith wants Calvin to stay in bed for three or four days at least, but he's ready to get up on the morning of day two. He's got bandages around his head and around his ribs. His face and lips have improved a little bit.

Katie tries to keep him in the bed, but Calvin pushes himself to a sitting position on the edge of the bed. Katie puts her hands on his shoulders to keep him sitting, but he growls and pushes her hands away. When he tries to stand up, his head whirls around and around on the inside, and he sits back down on his own.

"You need to lay back down, darling, you need more rest."

Calvin steadies himself and says, "We need to talk."

"What about?" Katie asks.

"Why don't you sit down, Katie." He waits till she sits before continuing. "Well, first of all, you assured me this place wasn't haunted …"

"I beg your pardon. I said I had heard stories, but I swear I haven't seen Pappy since he died."

"Well, I've seen your granddaddy twice in two days time. He was here before Big Ike's guys came to get me yesterday. He more or less warned me they were coming.

And I saw him out on the road two days ago when I first saw this place. He told me it was haunted. I guess he knew what he was talking about."

Calvin chuckles at his little joke, but it hurts his ribs so he stops. He looks at Katie. Her face is ashen. "Are you all right?"

"I don't know, Calvin. Are you mad at me?"

"Yeah, sort of. It scared the hell out of me, Katie, when I reached for him and got nothing but air."

"I thought you were a big hero and not afraid of no ghost."

"Well, it's one thing to say you ain't afraid of ghosts, and another to reach out for someone and get nothin'. That sure beats the only St. Elmo's fire I ever saw. But listen here. You're trying to change the subject."

"Will you ever forgive me?" She pleads.

"Probably, but first I want to know about you and Ike Drogue. I got my ass kicked up there after telling him I'm gonna marry you. He seems to think he's your fiancé, and he's convinced you know somethin' about a treasure Pappy buried somewhere around here."

"I know people been lookin' for buried treasure on my farm, and that's all I know," Katie says. "And look here, Calvin Cheeseburgers, I hate Big Ike Drogue. He's been pestering me to marry him ever since Pappy died. If he and I were the last two people left alive on this here earth, I wouldn't marry him. I'd move to The Middle of Nowhere before I'd marry that old cuss."

"You could have told me," Calvin says with as much innocence as he can muster.

"I don't think we've hardly had time to talk about our old boyfriends and girlfriends. But I think we could right now if you want to?"

Calvin thinks about all those women in all those cow towns and decides he doesn't want to know about her old boyfriends.

"I need to get back in the bed," he says, helpless all of a sudden. "I'm startin' to hurt again."

Katie helps him back into the bed, gets him a glass of water to take a pain pill, and then tucks him in. Calvin is exhausted. She kisses him on the bridge of his nose. "I love you," she says.

He is already asleep.

12

"Hey Calvin, wake up. Ya wanna play some poker?"

Calvin wakes up. Pappy is standing beside his bed leaning over him. "Ya wanna play some poker? Hayes's here. Couple of other guys, too."

"Yeah, sure," he says, getting out of the bed. He doesn't hurt anymore. He's not wearing bandages. He's wearing a suit and a bolo tie. "I love to play poker."

He's in the Silver Dollar Saloon in Austin. He follows Pappy through the crowd to a poker table with three men seated at it. Hayes is there, Hank Wilson from the bank, and Andy, the bank messenger. All five of them are dressed like ... well, dudes. They have on suits and bolo ties. The room is filled with cigar smoke, conversation, the tinkle of glass, and a piano player playing a piano.

The poker game proceeds, and conversation picks up around the table.

"That granddaughter of mine is going to make some young man a fine wife," Pappy says.

"I'm gonna marry her," Calvin speaks up.

"Are you sure about that, son? I hear tell she's gonna marry up with Mr. Big Ike."

"That ain't so, Pappy. She doesn't want Mr. Big Ike.

She wants me. She told me so."

"I think she should marry Calvin," Andy says. "He's much nicer than Ike."

"Listen," Hank pitches. "She should marry Big Ike. The two of them are among my biggest depositors. If they put their money together they would be really rich."

"He's much too old for her," Pappy says. "She needs a young man like ol' Calvin, here. The most important thing is that she be happy. Happiness is all I really want for her."

"I'll maker her happy, Pappy, I promise," Calvin says.

"She's a wildcat, son. Are sure you can handle a strong-willed woman? What if she goes off after Mr. Big Ike to shoot him for what he did to you? What would you do if she gets locked up in a storeroom up there at the Stockyard Cafe? You got the cajones to get her back from that the old sum bitch?"

13

Damn, damn, damn, Katie McGhee thinks. *What have I gotten myself into this time? I didn't even get off a shot, and now I'm locked in this goddamned storeroom.*

She pushes and pulls on the door, but it's locked and it ain't gonna budge. There are no windows, the only light coming in from around the door. Bags of flour, salt, pepper, baking soda, corn meal, and so on sit on shelves all around the room. Brooms, mops, buckets and cleaning supplies fill a corner. Several wooden barrels sit stacked in another corner.

What am I going to do? She asks herself. *Calvin is going to need me soon. I have to get back to Calvin.*

She bursts into tears. *There's no tellin' what Big Ike is going to do to me for pulling a gun on him. Damn, I didn't even get off a shot.*

"Girl, you sure got yourself in a fine fix. I had a feelin' something was wrong."

"Oh Granny, I'm so glad to see you. I've never been in such a fix, and I don't know what to do."

She wants to hug her granny, but she knows from experience there is nothing there to hug.

Her granny looks around the storeroom. This time

she's wearin' a camouflaged military fatigue uniform, a floppy brimmed field hat, and combat boots. She turns back to Katie and says, "Ok, child, fill me in on the action so far. What's happenin'?"

"You're talkin' funny again, Granny. As near as I can tell you're asking me why I'm locked in this here storeroom?"

"That's very good, dear, you're catchin' on."

Katie launches into her story about getting herself engaged to Calvin, but her granny stops her—

"Are you sure about this guy? You just met him yesterday?" Granny is looking over the storeroom with a flashlight from her utility belt.

"I've never been more sure of anything in all my life. I love him, Granny. That's why I'm here. I came here to shoot Big Ike for having Calvin beat up, but I never got off a shot. His goons, probably the guys who beat up Calvin, grabbed me and locked me in this here storeroom."

"Well, I'm glad you feel so strongly about Calvin. I got a good feelin' about him. Listen, girl, I was watchin' a rerun of MacGyver on TV the other night ..."

"You were doin' what?" Katie asks. "What is Tee Vee?"

"That doesn't matter, but what does is that I know how to get you out of here. Drag one of those barrels out from the wall. Now grab one of those buckets over there and let's take a look at what we got to work with here."

Katie follows her granny's instructions. They look

over the storeroom with Granny's flashlight like a couple of future Walmart shoppers.

Granny says, "Do you know why they call Ike Drogue, Big Ike?"

"No," Katie says.

"His package is huge."

"His package?" Katie asks.

"He has a big schwance."

"Look, Granny, you're talkin' funny again, and I don't know what you mean."

"I'm sorry, dear, I keep forgetting. He has a big cock."

Katie wonders how her granny knows this, and at the same time, she doesn't want to know.

14

"Wake up, Mr. Cheeseburgers, wake up."

Calvin opens his eyes and sees Allison, Katie's assistant, looking down at him. He's not sure if she's real or a dream. He reaches out and touches her hand.

Allison draws away. "Mr. Cheeseburgers, you're engaged to Miz Katie."

"I'm sorry, Allison, but I had an awful dream. I wasn't sure whether you were real or not."

"Do you know where Miz Katie is? She didn't come back from lunch. She came down here to see about you at lunchtime. Is she still here? Where is she? Nobody has seen her. I'm worried."

Calvin sits up. "I know where she is. I gotta get up to the Stockyard Cafe right now." Calvin swings his legs over the side of the bed, sits up, and stays there until his head stops spinning. He stands up in his long johns and walks to his chiffon robe and digs out his denim pants, a shirt, socks, and his boots.

"Mr. Cheeseburgers, you need to stay in bed," Allison says. She's afraid to touch him, so restraining him is out of the question.

Calvin dresses, takes a gun from a desk drawer, shoves

it in the waist of his pants, and leaves. He walks up the road toward the Stockyard Cafe, but people aren't so friendly this time. They get out of his way, and then stop and turn to watch him. No one speaks to him or tips their hats when they see the grim look on his face.

"Where you goin' boy?" Pappy says, walking next to him. "What the hell are you fixin' to do?"

"I'm goin' after Katie. Big Ike's got her locked up in a storeroom, and I'm gonna get her outta there. I'll kill Ike Drogue if I have to."

"Boy, you don't look so good. You're still green around the gills. You should be back home in bed. Do you even know how to use that piece you're totin'?"

"I was a soldier, Pappy, I joined up with the Union Army in New York City toward the end of the war, saw lots of dead soldiers. I'm gonna get Katie out of that storeroom."

"I'm a goin' with you, son, 'cause I don't rightly know that you're gonna make it."

"I'm okay, Pappy, I'll shoot Mr. Big Ike dead if I have to."

Calvin is slowing down. He's sweating. His chest hurts. His head throbs. But he walks on. His bandages are coming unwrapped and flapping. He walks along carrying on a conversation with someone no one else can see.

"The man is obviously coming undone," somebody says.

"He's gone round the bend," somebody else says.

"You think you've got problems with Big Ike? That sum bitch killed me," Pappy says. "He knocked me over the head in the back room of my own restaurant, dragged me up to the stockyards, and pushed me face down in a fresh cow pile. I really would like to see you kill Big Ike, but you gotta think about Katie. You two have a bright future ahead of you. Katie comes first. You gotta make sure Katie is okay …

When they reach the Stockyard Cafe, Calvin is ready to collapse. People are all about, but they are not interested in helping him.

"This is a job for the sheriff," somebody says.

Somebody else says, "Somebody call the sheriff."

Pappy directs Calvin through an alley between the Stockyard Offices and the Stockyard Cafe to another alley at the rear of the buildings. Big Ike steps from a door at the rear of the café.

"Well, well, Mr. Cheeseburgers, I told you to get out of town, and here you are."

"You better let Katie go, or I'll …"

"You'll do what?"

Calvin collapses in a helpless heap. He's unconscious. Pappy watches in horror.

Big Ike laughs. He draws a gun from under his coat and walks over to Calvin. He points the gun down at his head. "I told you to leave town. You shoulda listened to me, Mr. Cheeseburgers. Now I'm gonna have to kill ya."

Before Ike Drogue can squeeze the trigger of his Colt .45, an explosion rips open a rear wall of the Stockyard Cafe. Louder than thunder, the explosion shatters the windows in the Stockyard Offices and the café, echoes off the walls, and shakes buildings halfway to The Middle of Nowhere. Wooden shrapnel at ground zero.

A fireball roars out of the Stockyard Cafe like cannon shot and incinerates Big Ike, burns him to a crisp.

Pappy lifts up off the ground, his hands and feet shoot out in search of something to hold onto, no doubt, and his hat flies off. His head jerks forward and his eyes pop out of their sockets, vibrating on fine wire springs. Big Ike turns to ashes before his very eyes and falls to the ground in a pile. Pappy gets pulled apart and disappears with a pop.

An odor similar to gunpowder fills the air. A cacophony of cow bawling and pig squealing goes up in the stockyards. The cows are ready to stampede, but they aren't at home on the range anymore. The pigs riot in their pens.

People come running to see what happened. Several gather around Calvin to see what they can do for him. He doesn't appear to be burned. Others look at the pile of ashes and talk among themselves about what it means. Still others look at the ragged hole in the café's rear wall and shake their heads.

When the smoke clears, Katie peeks from the big hole in the wall. She sees Calvin on the ground, jumps from the building, and runs to him.

"Somebody help me get him back home," she cries out.

15

Calvin Cheeseburgers recovers from the beating Ike Drogue's thugs gave him, but he has no memory of what happened behind the Stockyard Cafe that day. He doesn't even remember walking up there.

Katie McGhee doesn't know what to tell him. She feels sure he isn't going to believe a story about her long-dead grandmother saving his life.

Nobody much cares about Big Ike Drogue burnin' up. Sheriff Trover declares it an accident. He doesn't even call the coroner for an inquest. Big Ike's family says a few words over his ashes, and then lets the wind blow them away. That's what they think about the family patriarch.

Katie tells Trover her story about Big Ike locking her in the storeroom, but she omits the part about tryin' to shoot him, and omits the part about Granny blowin' a hole in that wall and killin' the old bastard. She has no idea what her granny mixed together to cause the fireball she shot out of a barrel like it was a cannon that burned up Big Ike, so she's telling the truth when she tells the Sheriff she doesn't know how it happened.

Sheriff Trover buys her story and closes the case.

Ike Jr. inherits the Drogue Empire. He doesn't want

to run the Stockyard Cafe or the stockyards. He dabbles in the Livestock Market, eventually losing the family's ill-gotten fortune.

Ike Jr. is a big guy, but people call him Little Ike. Katie went through school with him at the You're Now Here School. She knows exactly why people call him Little Ike.

«————————————————————————————————»

Calvin convalesces over the next week or so in his bed. Hayes comes to visit almost every day. They pick up their friendship right where they left off. They talk about cooking, running restaurants, and the old days on trail drives. Hayes tells his bear story for the 1400th time.

"I remembers one time way up in Monatany when a late spring snow storm hits," Hayes says. "We ain't goin' anywhere in that snow. Several of our cows freeze. The boss is afraid we might lose the whole herd. One of the guys kills a great big bear. That mother humper must have weighed a ton. The guys drag that beast over to the cook wagon and tell me to cook it up for them. They was lucky 'cause it ain't every day a man gets to cook a bear. I had already cooked up a couple my own self, so I knowed what to do. The first thing you do with a dead bear is cool it. If you wanna eat it, that is. If it hadn't been for that snow, I probably wouldn't done any more than skin the old sum bitch. But I went on to clean it, butcher it, and cook up some bear steaks, ribs, the liver and heart. If I had had some potatoes, carrots, turnips, and onions,

I would have cooked up a bear stew. That's the best way to eat bear."

"So you're cookin' up bear sandwiches?" Calvin interrupts for the 1400th time.

"Naw, I ain't had any bear meat to cook since I been at the café. I been cookin' ground beef patties and making sandwiches, though. They've become quite popular. They call them hamburger sandwiches. You ought to put them on your menu when you get this place opened. The only problem with them is the bread. I been puttin' onions, tomatos, lettuce, and pickles on them and the bread gets soggy."

"You need something like those rolls Katie makes for the Hotel Dining Room," Calvin says before drifting off to sleep. "I'll talk to her about it ..."

«————————————————————————»

Calvin opens his restaurant to immediate success. Cheeseburgers is open for lunch, dinner, and late nights, and it's nearly always packed with customers. He serves hamburger sandwiches, grilled cheese sandwiches, soups, stews, salads, plate lunches, and later, other sandwiches and desserts. In no time at all, he's competing with The Stockyard Cafe and the Hotel Dining Room.

Calvin is satisfied being a cook. He's as happy as a frog in a pond working in his very own restaurant. Cheeseburgers is the culmination of all the dreams he dreamed sleeping on the ground with his saddle for a pillow and all those goddamned cows nearby making cow noises: moos, bawls, whines, cries, rustles, etc. He doesn't miss those days getting up off the ground in the morning, or maybe the middle of the night, and trying to get his aching body stretched back into shape. But what he doesn't miss most of all is the sore ass he gets after riding all day long, day after day in the middle of nowhere. Many miles in the saddle have been hard on his old ass. He ain't even 30-years old yet, and he's realizing ridin' herd on these goddamned stupid cows is a young man's game.

«————————————————————————»

One morning over breakfast, Calvin tells Katie about the problems Hayes is having with his hamburger sandwiches.

"I've done a little experimenting, and the rolls you make for the Hotel Dining Room are not quite big enough. We need something bigger, something new, something that won't get soggy, or at least not as fast as a slice of bread."

"I know what you mean. I ate a hamburger sandwich at the Hotel the other day. I sure like them dressed, but I had to eat it real fast before the bread got too soggy to handle."

"Do you think you can bake something like dinner rolls only a little bigger?"

"Darling," she says, leaning to kiss him. "How

many times do I have to tell you I'm a baker. I can bake anything."

After they kiss, Calvin says, "Hey, while I'm thinking about it. I got people askin' for desserts. They're wantin' pie or cake, and sometimes cookies. If you bake some of that stuff for me, I can sell it."

"Of course, Darling. I'll get Allison started on it right away."

16

Katie and Calvin are busy after they get engaged, but they find time to get hitched at the You're Now Here First Congregational Church on a Saturday afternoon approximately four weeks after meeting. The reception is at the Hotel Dining Room, which Katie bought from The Hotel You're Now Here. She runs the place now, as well her bakery.

When Little Ike runs his family's ill-gotten fortune into the ground, he has only the Stockyard Cafe left to sell. Everything else is gone. Katie Cheeseburgers buys the café, to much fanfare. *The You're Now Here World Guardian* reports it on the front page, complete with photos.

After buying the Stockyard Cafe, Katie meets with the staff between the lunch hours and the evening hours when the place is closed.

"Nobody is going to lose their job," Katie reassures her staff. "Hayes will be the manager. I'm only planning one other change. I'm gonna take the ovens out of the kitchen here, and move them to the Hotel Dining Room. Two of the bakers are going with them, and the third is going to work at my bakery down there on

Main Street where I recently added another oven. The Bakery and the Hotel Dining Room are going to supply the café with bread now, and other baked goods. I also supply my husband's restaurant, which you all know as Cheeseburgers. Ok, if you don't have any questions, I'm gonna turn the meeting over to Hayes and get back to my office. Come and see me if you have any problems. I have an open door policy."

Katie's office is now in the back of Cheeseburgers. She moves Calvin and all his furniture into the house. She moves her office from the house to the restaurant, and she feels right at home there. She learned the business from her grandparents in that very building. Her office in Pappy's room takes a little gettin' used to, but she does. Calvin is almost always there, and she feels comfortable when he's around. If he's not behind the counter cookin' or talkin' to customers, he's out in the yard doin' something or another. One time he and Hayes, in their spare time, restore the building to the way it looked when Pappy was alive and it was Pappy's Wild West Cafe—with castle like turrets.

Calvin's not much of a businessman, so he's happy to turn over the business of running [CHEESEBURGERS] to his wife. And besides, it iasn't like she just up and takes it away from him. No, sir.

"Calvin," Katie says at the table after dinner one night. "I've noticed you're not a very good businessman. Don't get me wrong. I love you dearly and want to help you, but you are a better cook than you are a businessman. Why don't you let me take care of your business?"

"Okay," Calvin says without a thought. "I reckon Cheeseburgers is as much yours as it is mine, anyway. Why, woman, I don't care anything about you taking care of the books. Go ahead. I hate workin' with the books. Let me cook, let me go after supplies, let me keep the fire goin', let me wash those damned dishes, let me do anything but keep the books."

"So, it's okay if I take over the business part of Cheeseburgers?"

"I thought I just said so. You wanna shake on it?"

Calvin smiles real big and reaches across the table to shake hands with Katie.

She returns his smile, only hers is bigger and prettier, and she grabs his hand, plants her elbow and tries to wrestle Calvin's arm down on the table.

Startled, Calvin recovers quickly. He was a cowboy even if he never rode a rodeo. He gets elbow planted on the tabletop and stops her before she pins him. Lifts her arm slow like. Strong like he thought she'd be. When he gets her hand and arm, and his of course, straight up between them and starts pushing her arm down, she leans forward and kisses him right on the mouth with some tongue. He drops her hand, climbs on the table with her, pushes everything off the table, and makes love to her all over the table. Knocks over a chair.

Afterwards, they have to scrub the table before they

can even think about eating another meal on it.

The next morning at breakfast (ham, eggs, taters, bacon, biscuits) Katie explains to Calvin that he owns part of her businesses, just like she owns part of his, and all four of their businesses are doing real well.

"You can retire if you want to," she says.

"Naw, I ain't ready to retire."

Calvin ain't ready to retire, but he considers cutting back on his hours. He considers the idea of being at home on the front porch in a rocking chair waving at anybody who happens by. He's never known such leisure. Sometimes he falls asleep in the rocker reading a book—cookbook, of course. Cooling breezes rustle the leaves on the big maples in the front yard. His mama made him go to school through the 8th grade, which was as high as he could go in Bedbug. Then she sent him off to Richmond, Baltimore, Philadelphia, or New York City. She didn't care which. *You can do better, son ...*

"Calvin," Katie says. She smiles at her hubby sleeping in that old rocking chair he found in the attic. She touches his shoulder. "Calvin."

Calvin wakes up and smiles at Katie. "Hi, sweety, whatcha got cookin'?"

"I brought dinner from the Hotel Dining Room and some of those cookies you like from the bakery. Are you ready to eat?"

"Yes." Calvin closes the cookbook on his lap, gets up from the rocker, places the book in the rocker, and turns to Katie. "Come here," he says.

"What do you want?" She smiles. "I've got supper ready in the kitchen."

Calvin steps over to Katie and slips his arms around her waist, pulls her to him, kisses her lips, her sweeter-than-strawberry lips, loses himself in the kiss 'cause he's in love with his wife.

Katie slips her arms gently around his neck, kisses him, loses herself in the kiss—

"Katie," Calvin says when they come up for air. "You're my family now. I feel like I'm home. I love you."

"I love you too," Katie whispers. "You are home 'cause this old house is our home."

They gaze into each other's eyes, and the old electricity is still there generating love. They kiss some more. They make their way to the door kissing, into the house kissing, tangoing down the hall kissing all the way to their bedroom, closing the door behind them. They postpone their supper by 15 or 20 minutes.

Business is booming. Calvin has a staff now: cooks, waiters, waitresses, busboys, the whole schmear. He opens the place every morning—except for Monday—at six o'clock and cooks breakfast. On Monday morning, he drives Katie's flat bed wagon down to the farmer's market and buys for their restaurants (The Hotel Dining Room, Katie's Bakery, the Stockyard Cafe, and of course, his own place, Cheeseburgers.

But more and more, he's leaving after his morning

shift and has time on his hands, so he and Hayes explore the farm. They find the old pond Katie spoke of in a clearing in the woods, and they sit there and fish for hours on end on a weekday afternoon or a Saturday or Sunday afternoon. They cook up what they catch over a campfire and eat it on Katie's sourdough bread.

Calvin finds an old leather tent of Pappy's in the barn loft. He cleans it up and takes Katie on a weekend camping trip. Calvin drives the flat bed wagon out to the pond. The wagon is loaded down with supplies, more than they need for two days, but that's Katie. She has to be ready for anything. That night sitting in front of the campfire, they talk.

"Katie, do you think Pappy buried a treasure somewhere on this farm?"

"No, I don't, Cal. He never talked about a buried treasure. My granny never talked about one, either."

"Big Ike said the treasure was his, not Pappy's."

"Big Ike was an evil man," Katie interjects. "I have no idea why he thought there was a treasure in the first place, and I certainly don't know why he thought it was his. This whole buried treasure thing is a mystery to me."

"Hayes seems to think it's true."

"Oh Lordy," Katie says. "Sometimes I think he's as crazy as the man in the moon."

17

Calvin and Hayes build a cabin in the clearing next to the pond. They call it their vacation retreat. Katie suspects they're looking for a buried treasure, but they always invite her along, and sometimes she goes with them, so she's not sure. Katie enjoys Hayes' company, though she thinks he's crazy. He's full of wild stories about cooking for cowboys.

"You know," Hayes says. "I told the first part of the bear story 1400 times, but I've never had a chance to tell the end of it. Somebody always interrupts."

"Well, go ahead and tell it," Calvin says. Katie agrees. The three of them are sittin' around a campfire in the clearing near the pond under a starry sky. The story already smells as fishy as the pond.

"Well ok, I will. As you probably remember, we're up in Montany in a snow storm. Two or three head of cattle freeze to death. We gotta get them carcasses to market before they ruin on us. We got us this great big old bear skin, and I'm all for making it into a blanket, but the boss has other ideas. We've got to get these frozen cows to market, he says. We wrap the cows in the bear skin, tie it together with a rope in two places, and Rowdy and

Gil ride them like a sled down the hill to market. They ride off clutching the ropes around the bear skin, waving their hats, and yelling *Yippee* and *Yahoo* like they're riding a rodeo bull. They sail over the first hill, then the next, and they're out of sight. *Yippee* and *Yahoo* echoes back to us. We catch up with them in Hell Fer Sartin, a little town at the bottom of the mountain. The snow is gone, it's warmed up considerably, and Rowdy and Gil are sittin' on the veranda of the local cathouse drinkin' bottled beer with a couple of good lookin' cats. The boss takes the money what's left from the sale of the beef and buys beer for everybody, and fruits and vegetables, and flour. I cook up a batch of bear stew with our leftover bear meat. Half of that town lines up for a bowlful. And I bake up a batch of biscuits, too. A man's gotta have biscuits with his bear stew."

Katie can't go with Calvin and Hayes every time they invite her to the cabin. She's a busy woman making money running three restaurants and a bakery.

On a sunny summer Sunday afternoon, Calvin and Hayes are sittin' on the ground next to the pond fishin' and drinkin' beer.

"Whaddya think the treasure is?" Hayes asks for the 1400th time. "Ya think it's gold? Ol' Pappy made a fortune in Californie, you know. I bet there's thousands of dollars in gold buried somewhere on this farm. I sure would like to find it."

"Now Hayes, don't get no ideas about diggin' up this

farm. Katie would shoot you and me both. Besides, I hear tell they ain't no treasure."

"Where did you hear that?" Hayes responds. "Who tole you that?"

"Why Katie, of course." Calvin doesn't want to tell Hayes about Pappy.

"How does she know?" Hayes wants to know.

"Katie says Pappy put all of his money in the bank. Says Pappy never talked about buryin' a treasure, and her grandmother didn't either."

"Maybe Pappy didn't tell his own wife about the treasure. He was like that, you know."

"Now listen here, Hayes. I know you well enough to know that you're gonna dig around here looking for a treasure whether we want you to or not. So, don't let Katie know what yer up to. Don't leave any piles of dirt around here, or she'll let you have it with both barrels."

"Don't worry about me, Cal, I don't leave tracks."

"Hayes, when we were out there drivin' cattle, people used to say you was runnin' from the law for something you did back east. I've often wondered about that. Is it true. Are you runnin'?

"Not anymore. I wasn't runnin' from the law when I came west. I was runnin' from ghosts."

"Whaddya mean?" Calvin asks, startled.

"I lived in Baltimore before coming west. My wife and daughter died of influenza. The flu swept through the city in 1859. I don't know why I didn't get it. I was working in a restaurant, but I couldn't stand the loneliness at home anymore. I left Maryland and drifted for years. I wound up in Topeka somehow. I got a job cookin' for a wagon train, and then a cattle drive, and worked at that until I went to work for Big Ike. I didn't realize what a crook he was until after Pappy died.

Calvin catches a fish and pulls it in.

"I sure am sorry to hear about yer wife and daughter. That must have been awful."

"It sure was."

18

While Katie is in the office planning Pappy's Wild West Cafes for Central Kansas, Calvin is cookin' up hamburgers and serving them on Katie's hamburger buns. Cheeseburgers and the Stockyard Cafe are selling hamburgers like hotcakes. They're a smash hit on Katie's buns. Even the Hotel Dining Room is selling them. On a day in December 1872 with Christmas in the air, a cowboy wearing a long leather coat walks into Cheeseburgers when the lunch hour is almost over. He sits at the counter and tells Calvin what he wants.

"I want one of them cheeseburgers you got advertised on the front of the building."

"Excuse me," Calvin says. "A cheeseburger? I don't know what you—"

But Calvin stops. *Hmm, a cheeseburger.* "Hold on," he tells the guy. He goes to the icebox and opens it. About half a block of cheddar cheese sits there, big and yellow as you please. He hasn't sold many grilled cheese sandwiches since Tony quit. "Ok, one cheeseburger coming up. You want me to dress your burger? You know, run it through the garden."

"Yeah, run it through the garden. Put some of that

mustard on it, too. And give me a cup of joe. It's gettin' cold out there."

Calvin fries a hamburger in a skillet, and when it's almost ready, he puts a slice of cheese on it to let it melt a little. He toasts the bun in the skillet, each part face down. When the bun is toasty, he spreads mustard on half of it, mayonnaise on the other, and stacks a piece of lettuce, a slice of onion, pickles, and a slice of tomato on the mayonnaise half. Using a spatula, he scoops the world's very first cheeseburger off the skillet and places it on the garden stack. He tops it with the other half of the bun and delivers it to his customer.

The cheeseburger is an immediate hit. Cheeseburgers, The Stockyard Cafe, and The Hotel Dining Room can't sell them fast enough. People are coming all the way from The Middle of Nowhere to eat cheeseburgers. People are movin' to You're Now Here for cheeseburgers. Calvin is a celebrity. His cheeseburgers are everybody's first choice, but he can't serve everybody trying to get into his restaurant for a cheeseburger. The Stockyard Cafe and the Hotel Dining Room get the overflow, and surely I don't have to remind you who owns those two establishments.

The town is growing. New factories spring up on South Broadway manufacturing wagon wheels and harnesses and leather goods. A blacksmith builds a barn near the factories and opens the town's second blacksmith shop. An apothecary opens on South Broadway near the center of town

Henderson buys the You're Now Here Trading Post from the guy who bought it from Little Ike. He expands his original operation to include a farmer's market on South Broadway. He buys fresh fruits and vegetables from local farmers and sells them to the town's three restaurants, as well as the public.

Katie opens her first Pappy's Wild West Cafe on South Broadway. Calvin and Hayes help her build the place. It looks like the original Pappy's Wild West Cafe, which is now called Cheeseburgers. On the first day, the new restaurant sells more cheeseburgers than the other three restaurants all together. The folks working in the new factories and stores love cheeseburgers. They can't eat enough of them.

Over the next two or three years, Katie opens Pappy's Wild West Cafes all over central Kansas. She builds them with local labor, trains the employees, opens them, and then sells them to local interests. She is making money faster than she can haul it off to The You're Now Here State Bank in an armored wagon.

On the night of their third wedding anniversary, Calvin and Katie are sitting in the gazebo Calvin and Hayes built in the yard. They're digesting a big celebration dinner at the Hotel Dining Room, which is still the best restaurant in town and the flagship of Katie's empire.

Calvin says to Katie, "Hayes decided today that there ain't no buried treasure on the farm. He's been lookin' for several years now."

"I thought maybe he was," Katie says, "but I never saw any dirt piles out there like I used to, so I couldn't be sure. You were helpin' him, weren't you?"

"Yeah, I guess I was. Pappy told me there was no buried treasure, and you told me as much, but Hayes wouldn't believe me. He was fun to watch. Say, I haven't seen Pappy around the restaurant since Big Ike got himself burned up. It's been over three years."

"I haven't seen Granny since then, either."

"What?" Calvin says. "You never told me you've seen your dead granny."

"Are you sure 'bout that? Maybe you weren't listenin' to me. You do that sometimes, you know?"

"I don't think so. Surely, I would remember something like that."

"It doesn't matter. She told me once that she only came around when I needed her. I guess I don't need her anymore. And don't call me Shirley."

As always, Katie's humor hops right on over Calvin's head like a big ol' frog.

Katie smiles at Calvin and says, "I got you now, Cal."

She kisses away his puzzled look, and he replies, "And I got you, Katie."

ABOUT THE AUTHOR

Dean Crawford writes fiction and poetry. Over the years, he's actually published some of it, mostly in small literary magazines long gone and forgotten—except for Dean's copies, of course. Dean was born in Louisville, Kentucky a long time ago. He's graduate of the University of Kentucky with a BA in Journalism, which explains why he lives in Lexington, Kentucky with his wife, a dog and, a cat.